MY 1ST GRAPHIC NOVEL®

TOO SHORT FOR THE COURT

STONE ARCH BOOKS
a capstone imprint

My First Graphic Novels are published by Stone Arch Books
A Capstone Imprint
1710 Roe Crest Drive
North Mankato, Minnesota 56003
www.capstonepub.com

Library of Congress Cataloging-in-Publication Data
Lemke, Amy J.
Too short for the court / by Amy J. Lemke; illustrated by Steve Harpster.
p. cm. — (My first graphic novel)
Summary: Morgan loves to shoot hoops, but she is the smallest girl on her team—can her friend Alexis help her to think big before the next game?
ISBN 978-1-4342-3282-3 (library binding)
ISBN 978-1-4342-3862-7 (pbk.)
1. Basketball—Comic books, strips, etc. 2. Basketball stories. 3. Friendship—Comic books, strips, etc. 4. Friendship—Juvenile fiction. 5. Graphic novels. [1. Graphic novels. 2. Basketball—Fiction. 3. Friendship—Fiction.] I. Harpster, Steve, ill. II. Title. III. Series: My first graphic novel.
PZ7.7.L458To 2012
741.5'973—dc23

2011032216

Art Director: Bob Lentz
Graphic Designer: Brann Garvey
Production Specialist: Michelle Biedscheid

Printed in the United States of America in Stevens Point, Wisconsin.
102011
006404WZS12

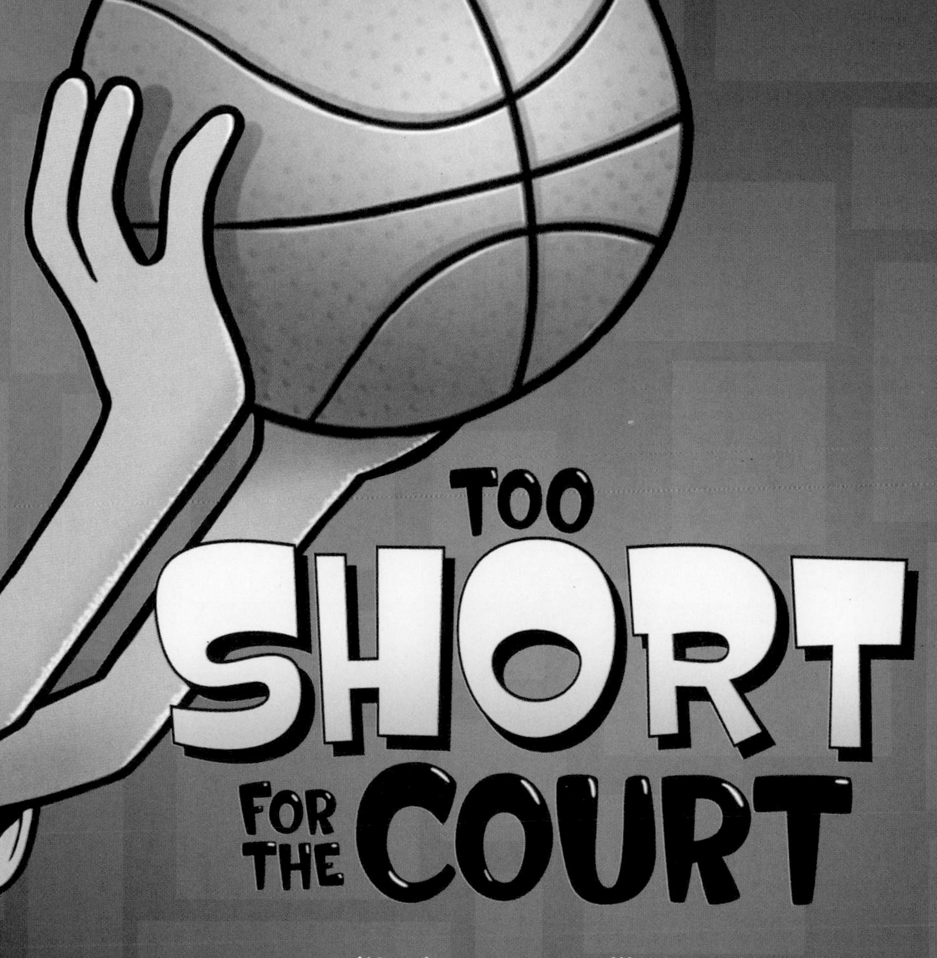

Too Short for the Court

written by
Amy J. Lemke

illustrated by
Steve Harpster

HOW TO READ A GRAPHIC NOVEL

Graphic novels are easy to read. Boxes called panels show you how to follow the story. Look at the panels from left to right and top to bottom.

Read the word boxes and word balloons from left to right as well. Don't forget the sound and action words in the pictures.

1 After that, Nico came to practice on time. He worked on his batting.

4 He was ready to catch the ball when it came his way.

The pictures and the words work together to tell the whole story.

Morgan's favorite thing to do is play basketball.

She shoots hoops every day.

She shoots hoops every night.

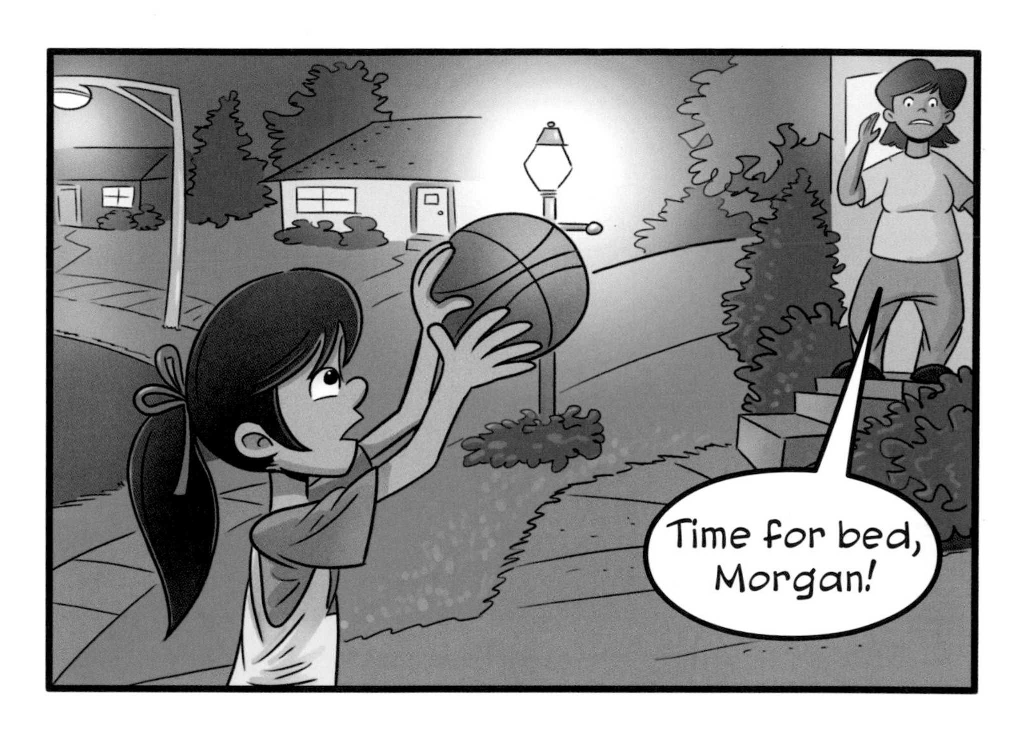

But on the school team, she gets lost in the crowd.

CUBS
I'm right here, Coach!

During games, Morgan's passes get stolen. Her shots get blocked.

Even so, her team hasn't lost a single game.

They are going to play the Tigers for the championship.

Not that Morgan cares.

Morgan's friend Alex knows that something is wrong.

Alex wants to help. She hates seeing Morgan so sad.

The next day, Morgan and Alex practice together.

Instead of working on free throws, they shoot over tall ladders.

Come on!

BANG

Instead of dribbling around cones, they weave through giant trees.

They practice bounce passes on the four-square court.

The day of the championship, Morgan is ready.

But the Tigers are ready as well.

Morgan and Alex cannot believe how tall the Tiger players are.

During the game, Morgan's team stays close.

Morgan's extra practice pays off.

She keeps her head up and aims high.

The game is tied. With one second left on the clock, Morgan is fouled.

One shot could win the game. Size doesn't matter.

It's the days and nights of practice that count.

Morgan makes her shot!

The Cubs win!

Being on top for once feels pretty good.

BIOGRAPHIES

AMY J. LEMKE is an early childhood special education teacher in Cambridge, Minnesota. She lives with her husband, Donnie, her puppy, Paulie, and her cat, Dylan. When Amy was younger, she played basketball. Just like her character Morgan, Amy was always the "short one on the team." Today, Amy enjoys going for bike rides, camping, traveling, and taking pictures.

STEVE HARPSTER has loved drawing funny cartoons, mean monsters, and goofy gadgets since he was able to pick up a pencil. Now he does it for a living. Steve lives in Columbus, Ohio, with his wonderful wife, Karen, and their sheepdog, Doodle.

GLOSSARY

BOUNCE PASSES (BOUNSS PASS-ez) — a type of basketball pass that hits the floor before reaching the receiver

CHAMPIONSHIP (CHAM-pee-uhn-ship) — a contest or final game of a series that determines which team or player will be the overall winner

DRIBBLING (DRIB-uhl-ing) — in basketball, bouncing the ball while running, keeping it under control

FOULED (FOULD) — performed an action in sports that is against the rules

FREE THROWS (FREE THROHS) — in basketball, open shots made from behind a set line

STOLEN (STOHL-in) — when the ball is stolen in basketball, it has been taken away from the dribbler by a player from the other team

DISCUSSION QUESTIONS

1. Morgan thought she was too short to be good at basketball. Have you ever thought you wouldn't be good at something because of your size? What was it?

2. Do you think Morgan was a good teammate? Why or why not?

3. Morgan needed extra practice to be ready for the championship game. What sort of things have you practiced for?

WRITING PROMPTS

1. How did Alex help Morgan? Write a list of the different ways.

2. Morgan's favorite thing to do is playing basketball. Draw a picture of yourself doing your favorite thing. Then write a sentence that explains your picture.

3. Throughout the book, there are sound and action words next to some of the art. Pick at least two of those words. Then write a sentence using those words.

MY FIRST GRAPHIC NOVEL

These books are the perfect introduction to the world of safe, appealing graphic novels. Each story uses familiar topics, repeating patterns, and core vocabulary words appropriate for a beginning reader. Combine the entertaining story with comic book panels, exciting action elements, and bright colors and a safe graphic novel is born.

Casey did not want to go swimming.

Water might get in her eyes and up her nose. Her hair would get wet.

6

Then Casey saw the new pool at the sports center. It looked so fun.

7

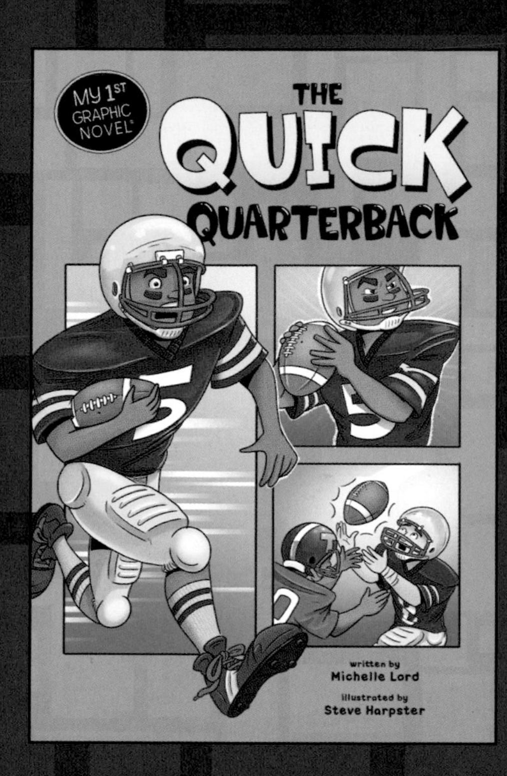
MY 1ST GRAPHIC NOVEL
THE QUICK QUARTERBACK
written by
Michelle Lord
illustrated by
Steve Harpster

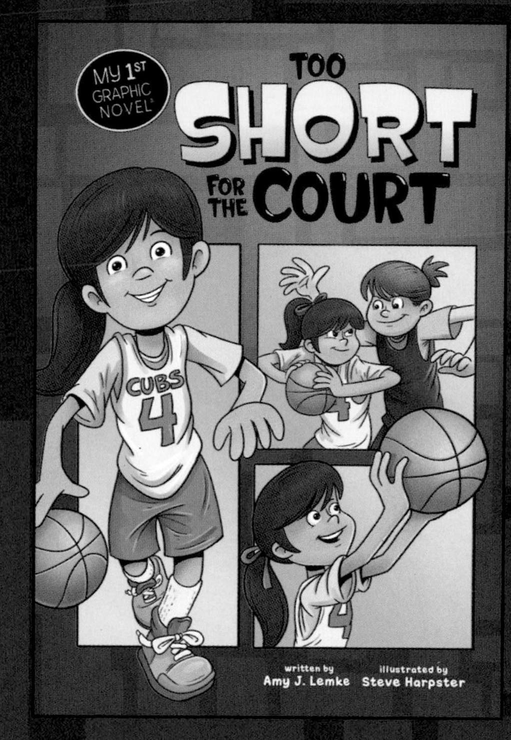
MY 1ST GRAPHIC NOVEL
TOO SHORT FOR THE COURT
CUBS 4
written by
Amy J. Lemke
illustrated by
Steve Harpster

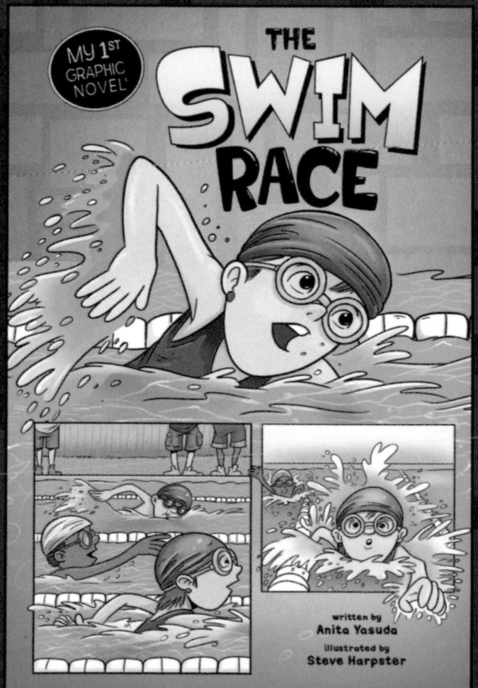
MY 1ST GRAPHIC NOVEL
THE SWIM RACE
written by
Anita Yasuda
illustrated by
Steve Harpster

MY 1ST GRAPHIC NOVEL
FIRST BASE BLUES
written by
Anita Yasuda
illustrated by
Steve Harpster

THE FUN DOESN'T STOP HERE!

DISCOVER MORE AT...

WWW.CAPSTONEKIDS.COM